COUNTRY TALES

BY

BEATRIX POTTER

™

Illustrated by

PAULINE BAYNES

FREDERICK WARNE

FREDERICK WARNE

Penguin Books Ltd, Harmondsworth, Middlesex, England
Viking Penguin Inc., 40 West 23rd Street, New York, New York 10010, U.S.A.
Penguin Books Australia Ltd, Ringwood, Victoria, Australia
Penguin Books Canada Ltd, 2801 John Street, Markham, Ontario, Canada L3R 1B4
Penguin Books (N.Z.) Ltd, 182–190 Wairau Road, Auckland 10, New Zealand

First published by Frederick Warne in *The Fairy Caravan*, 1929
This edition first published 1987

Copyright © Frederick Warne & Co., 1929, 1987

ISBN 0 7232 3447 7

Typeset by CCC, printed and bound in Great Britain by
William Clowes Limited, Beccles and London

CONTENTS

INTRODUCTION

THE three stories in this book were first published in 1929 as part of *The Fairy Caravan*, by Beatrix Potter. It describes a miniature circus, composed of a group of animals who travel the country together, shielded from human eyes by magic fernseed. They tell various tales along the way, and are in turn entertained by the animals they meet.

The first story here is told by Xarifa the dormouse to the long-haired guinea-pig Tuppenny, whilst they are sewing a robe for Tuppenny's forthcoming appearance in the circus. The second comes from the ewe Tibbie Woolstockit, who lives in the field where the circus pitches camp. Habbitrot, another sheep, provides the final story, of the spinner after whom she was named.

Beatrix Potter was urged to write *The Fairy Caravan* by David Mackay, a publisher from Philadelphia. It is a deeply personal book that reveals her great love of the Lake District countryside and its animal inhabitants. Her preface to *The Fairy Caravan* provides a fitting introduction to this volume also :

"As I walked by myself,
And talked to myself,
Myself said unto me—
    Through many changing seasons these tales have walked and talked with me. They were not meant for printing ; I have left them in the homely idiom of our old north country speech. I send them on the insistence of friends beyond the sea."

LITTLE MOUSE

LITTLE Mouse was asked to a wedding. And she said "What shall I wear? What shall I wear? There is a hole in my old gray gown, and the shops are shut on a Wednesday."

And while Little Mouse was wondering there came to the door of her little house an old buff green-striped caterpillar man, with a band across his shoulder and a pack upon his back. And he sang, "Any tape, any buttons, any needles, any pins? Any hooks, any eyes, any silver safety-pins? Any ribbons, any braid, any thread of any shade, any fine spotty muslin today, M'mm?"

He turned the band over his head and stood the pack open on the doorstep, and showed Little Mouse his wares. And she bought fine spotty muslin from the caterpillar man. Little Mouse spread the muslin on her table, and she cut out a mob-cap and tippet. Then she said "I have scissors and thimble and needles and pins; but no thread. How shall I sew it? How shall I sew it?"

Then by good luck there came to the door of her house a hairy brown spider with eight little eyes. He, too, had a pack, a tin box on his back; and his name was Webb Spinner. He sang "Spinneret, spinneret! the best you can get! Reels and bobbins, bobbins and reels! White thread and black, the best in my pack! Come buy from Webb Spinner!" So Little Mouse bought white thread, and she sewed her cap and tippet.

And while Little Mouse was sewing, a large moth came to the door, selling— "Silk, spun silk! Silk spun fine! Woven by the silk moth, who'll buy silk of mine?" Her silk was apple-green, shot with thread of gold and silver; and she had gold cord, and silken tassels, too. Little Mouse bought silk enough to make herself a gown, and she trimmed it with gold cord and tassels.

And when she was dressed, attired all in her best, she said—"How can I dance? how can I dance with the Fair Maids of France, with my little bare feet?"

Then the wind blew the grass and whispered in the leaves; and the fairies brought Little Mouse a pair of lady's slippers. And Little Mouse danced at the wedding.

Daisy and Double

DAISY and Double were twin lambs who grazed in the pastures. The coppice has been cut thrice since then; but still the green shoots grow again from the stools, and the bluebells ring in the wood. And Wilfin Beck sings over the pebbles, year in and year out, and swirls in spring flood after the melting snow. That April when Daisy and Double played in this meadow, Wilfin was full to overflowing, as high `as it is now. Take care! you thoughtless lambs, take care!

But little heed took Daisy and Double, who made of the flood a playmate. For it was carrying down sticks and brown leaves and snow-broth—as the trout-fishers call the cakes of white fairy foam that float upon the flood water in early spring. Daisy and Double saw the white foam; and they thought it was fun to race with the snow-broth; they on the meadowbank and the foam upon the water; until it rushed out of sight behind this wall. Then back they raced upstream till they met more snow-broth coming down; then turned and raced back with it.

But they watched the water instead of their own footsteps—splash! in tumbled Daisy. And before he could stop himself—splash! in tumbled Double; and they were whirled away in the icy cold water of Wilfin Beck. "Baa! baa!" cried Daisy and Double, bobbing along amongst the snow-broth. Very sadly they bleated for their mother; but she had not seen them fall in. She was feeding quietly, by herself. Presently she missed them; and she commenced to run up and down, bleating. They had been carried far away out of sight, beyond the wall; beyond another meadow.

Then Wilfin Beck grew tired of racing; the water eddied round and round in a deep pool, and laid the lambs down gently on a shore of smooth sand. They staggered onto their feet and shook their curly coats—"I want my mammy! baa, baa!" sobbed Daisy. "I'm very cold, I want my mammy," bleated Double. But bleat as they might, their mother Dinah Woolstockit could not hear them.

The bank above their heads was steep and crumbly. Green fronds of oak-fern were uncurling; primroses and wood anemones grew amongst the moss, and yellow catkins swung on the hazels. When the lambs tried to scramble up the bank—they rolled back, in danger of falling into the water. They bleated piteously. After a time there was a rustling amongst the nut bushes; some-one was watching them.

This person came walking slowly along the top of the bank. It wore a woolly shawl, pulled forward over its ears, and it leaned upon a stick. It seemed to be looking straight in front of it as it walked along; at least its nose did; but its eyes took such a sharp squint sideways as it passed above the lambs. "Burrh! burrh!" said this seeming woolly person with a deep-voiced bleat. "Baa! baa! We want our mammy!" cried Daisy and Double down below.

"My little dears come up! burrh! burrh! come up to me!" "Go away!" cried Daisy, backing to the water's edge. "You are not our mammy! Go away!" cried Double. "Oh, real mammy, come to us!" Then the woolly person reached out a skinny black arm from under the shawl, and tried to claw hold of Daisy with the handle of its stick. Its eyes were sharp and yellow, and its nose was shiny black. "Baa, baa!" screamed Daisy, struggling, and rolling down the bank, away from the crook. "Burrh! burrh! bad lambs; I'll have you yet!"

But what was that noise? A welcome whistle and shout—"Hey, Jack, good dog! go seek them out, lad!" The wily one threw off the shawl and ran, with a long bushy tail behind him; and a big strong wall-eyed collie came bounding through the coppice, on the track of the fox. When he came to the top of the bank, he stopped and looked over at Daisy and Double with friendly barks. Then John Shepherd arrived, and came slithering down the bank between the nut bushes. He lifted up Daisy and Double, and carried them to their mother.

HABBITROT

LONG, long ago, long before the acorn ripened that has grown into yonder oak—there lived a bonny lass at the farm in the dale, and a yeoman from Brigsteer came to court her.

Her parents were willing for the match, and Bonny Annot liked the yeoman well; a brave, handsome fellow and a merry. He had sheep on the fell, cows in the byre, a horse in the stall, a dry flag-roofed house, and many a broad acre. For dower her father would give her a cow and a heifer, a score of sheep, and ten silver crowns.

Her mother would give her her blessing ; but not without shame and a scolding. Now this was the trouble—two elder daughters when they married had had great store of blankets and sheets. For it was a good old custom in the dale that all practical lasses should spin flax and wool, and have the yarn woven by the webster, so that they had ready against their bridewain a big oak bedding chest well filled with linen and blankets.

But this youngest daughter, Bonny Annot, was both the laziest and the bonniest ; not one pound of wool had she carded, not one hank of flax had she spun! "Shut thee in the wool loft with thy spindle ; go spin, idle Annot, go spin!"

Bonny Annot spun from morning till noon, from noon till the shadows grew long. But it was late a-day to commence to spin. "My back is tired, my fingers are stiff, my ears they drum with the hum of the wheel. Oh well and away to Pringle Wood, to meet my love," in the gloaming. She left her wheel, she lifted the latch, she stole away while the cows were milking.

In Pringle Wood across the beck the hazels grew as still they grow, and wind flowers and violets and primroses twinkled. Bonny Annot wandered through the wood, she knelt on the moss to gather a posey ; and herself was the sweetest of flowers that grow.

Blue were her eyes like the wood violet's blue, fair were her locks like the mary-bud's gold, and her red-and-white dimples like roses on snow! She bent to the flowers and she heard a low humming. Was it horse's hoofs on the fell road from Brigsteer? Trot, trot, habbi-trot, trot, trot, trot, trot, trot! She lifted her head and she listened; but no. She knelt on the moss and again she heard humming; was it bumbly bees storing their honey below? She peeped between stones and mossy hazel stumps, beneath a hollow stone, beneath a mossy stump—and there underground she saw a wee wee woman spinning—hum, hum! went her wheel; spinning, spinning, spinning.

"Hey, Bonny Annot!" said the little gray woman, "why art thou so pale and heavy-eyed?"

"With spinning, good woman, with spinning!"

"Spinning is for winter nights, Bonny Annot; why spinnest thou now, in the pleasant spring?" "Because I was idle, I now must spin in haste. Alack! my sheets and blankets are to spin." She told her tale and cried.

"Dry your eyes and listen, Bonny Annot," said the little gray woman, "eyes so blue and tender were never meant for tears. Lazy thou may be, but I know thee kind and true. Step up to the wool-loft in the moonlight; tie the bags of flax and wool upon the pony; bring them to old Habbitrot, and she will do thy spinning!"

Even while Annot thanked her there came the clink of horseshoes along the stony road from Brigsteer; Bonny Annot forgot her troubles and sprang to meet the yeoman.

But when he rode away next morning her troubles recommenced—her mother, with a hazelrod, drove her up the steps to the loft. "It wants but three weeks to thy wedding—go spin, idle daughter, go spin!" Many were the fleeces and the bags of wool and flax. So many that when she took away a load upon her pony—the wool was never missed; not although she made four journeys to and fro from Pringle Wood. "Bring more, bring more to old Habbitrot! Thou shalt have wealth of sheets and blankets!"

Down below under the hollow stone there was the noise of spinning; hum, hum, trot, trot, trot! habbitrot, trot, trot!

Little way made Bonny Annot with her own spinning in the wool-loft; yet she sang while she turned the wheel. What though the thread broke and the flax was lumpy, still she sang and laughed while she spun. In the evening she stole away once more to Pringle Wood, riding barebacked on her pony— "Lead him to the Colludie Stone! Up with the bags and bundles! Wealth for thy wedding, Bonny Annot; she that spoke kindly to old Habbitrot shall never want for blankets."

Bonny Annot's mother expected but little in the morning. She climbed up to the wool-loft with the broomstick in her hand—"Say hast thou spun e'er a pound of wool, or a hank of flax, lazy daughter?"

Wonders will never cease! which of her sisters had ever had such yarn for the weaver? Worsted so strong and even; or thread so fine and fair? Her fame as a spinner was spread beyond the dale; it came to the ears of the yeoman. He, too, had great store of white wool and flax. Said her mother, "See what a housewife thou art marrying! Surely she will fill thy linen-press and deck thy cupboard!" But Bonny Annot hung her head and pouted her lip; thought she— "He will keep me at spinning forever."

The wedding day came. They were a handsome pair. The sun shone; the bells were rung; all the folk in the dale came to the kirk to see them married. And the wedding feast at the farm was thronged and merry. The trenchers were piled with meat; there were cakes and pies and pasties; the jugs of ale went round, and Bonny Annot kissed the cup.

Someone knocked at the house-door. The bride sprang to open it. At her feet upon the threshold stood a little ugly woman, a little gray old woman, with a kindly crooked smile.

"Good dame, come in! Welcome to my wedding feast!" Bonny Annot led her to the table, set chair and footstool and cushion, filled trencher and cup. The weddingers looked askance at the unbidden guest; they pointed and they whispered. But still the bonny bride served her, filling trencher and cup. The old woman munched, and munched, and munched. Now the bride's youngest brother was a merry knave, "Hey, little woman!" said he, "why hast thou such an ugly ugly mouth, wide and awry with a long flabby lip?" "Whisht, whisht, Henry!" said Bonny Annot, pulling him.

The little woman smiled awry—
"With spinning, my lad, with spinning."
She wet her finger on her ugly flabby
lip, and made as if she twisted thread;
her thumb was broad and flat.

"Oh ho!" said the yeoman, "is *that*
what comes of spinning?" He kissed
Bonny Annot's cherry lips and tapered
fingers, "Oh ho! so that comes of spinning?"

The old woman munched and
munched and munched. "Hey, little
woman," said Henry, "why is thy back
so bent, thine eyes so bleared, and thy
foot so flat?"

"With spinning, my lad, with spinning!" She beat her broad foot up and down upon the flags as though she trod the treadle—trot, trot, Habbitrot, trot, trot, trot, trot, trot!

"So ho!" said the yeoman, who was very fond of dancing, "so ho, Habbitrot! if *that* comes of spinning—my wife's foot shall never treadle. No, no, Habbitrot! When *we* have wool and flax to spin, my wife shall dance and sing. We will send for Habbitrot! Habbitrot shall do our spinning; we will send for Habbitrot."